THE CITY OF SHADES

ANAÏS BLUE
PREQUEL

by PJ Whittlesea

Published by Tyet Books, Amsterdam
www.tyetbooks.com
information@tyetbooks.com

Ordering Information: Quantity sales. Special discounts are available on quantity purchases by corporations, associations, and others. For details, contact the "Special Sales Department" at the address above.

Cover designed by MiblArt

Also by P J Whittlesea
Loreless
Paperback ISBN: 978-94-92523-00-6
Hardcover ISBN: 978-94-92523-05-1

For Nan

Music is Magic ... Magic is Life ...

Jimi Hendrix, 1942-1970

Prologue - The Concert

Mick Jagger gyrated his hips and spat into the microphone. He screamed at the audience to raise their hands. They obliged, clapping in unison with the singer. The stage lights panned over his body. They cut harsh shadows from his thin frame. He looked much younger than he was. The lighting shaved years off him.

The colossus above and around the stage dwarfed the band. The scenery, constructed of massive steel girders, looked like a gigantic Meccano set. From her position in the wings, Anaïs Blue heard compressed air hiss from the hydraulics powering the theatrical scenery. Great metal elements swung above her head and slotted into place, forming a new backdrop. A giant video screen, centre-stage, flickered and beamed out images of war and suffering.

Charlie Watts struck up a steady rhythm. Keith arched his neck and leaned back, his guitar swaying loosely around his hips. He spat out his cigarette, blew a cloud of smoke into the air and stamped out the butt. The cinders flew up around his boot. In one swift movement he pulled a fresh cigarette seemingly out of nowhere. He flipped it into his mouth and a roadie rushed from the wings to ignite it.

Anaïs had drugged a mountain of a security guard. He hovered by her side. Together they watched the band explode into their next song: 'Paint it black'. From her perch at the side of the stage Anaïs had a bird's-eye view of the audience below. A mass of colour, punctuated by bobbing heads, swept out beneath her and far into the distance. A spotlight, ensconced atop a tower in the middle of the throng, blinded her as it panned across the stage and caught her in its beam. She ducked behind the security guard for shelter.

The park was full to bursting. People sat on the shoulders of others to get a better view. They punched the air. Flags and banners stuck out of the mass. As the song began the multitude lurched forward in unison with the beat. The banners flapping in the wind gave the impression the crowd was an army charging into battle. As the crowd surged forward, people sandwiched in the front row were pressed up against the barriers. They fought for breath.

Anaïs watched as two security guards pulled a small girl out of the crowd and doused her in water. She could not have been much older than Anaïs's own physical self—five years of age. The little girl fell limp in their arms. Her eyes glazed over and Anaïs knew the potion had kicked in. She had spiked the water and the child would now be seeing purple. Anaïs smiled in satisfaction.

The surging chug of guitars and bass built to a crescendo. Anaïs shut her eyes. She listened to the music. It was good. It enveloped her. She reached out a hand and felt the towering speaker stack beside her. The vibrations ran up her arm and sent a buzz through her body. The rumbling bass made the stage under her shoes quiver. She floated on the ripples of sound and let the reverberations turn her body to jelly. Anaïs's grin widened. Nan would be jealous.

Anaïs had lost her caretaker in the labyrinth of the makeshift village in the backstage area. Lost was not entirely correct. She had given her the slip. She knew that she should be looking for Nan. It had not been the right thing to do, ditching her like that, but she wanted some time alone. She would look for her later. Right now, she just wanted to bask in the moment. Once Nan found her there would be trouble. It was worth it, though.

She opened her eyes and looked down into the audience again. Nice! Just like the little girl who had been pulled from the crowd, the eyes of the audience in the front row had glazed over. The effect of the potion was fanning out from this central point. Even the security personnel at the foot of the stage were gaping in awe. *Cool, it's working.*

In the middle of the stage a movement caught her eye. Two stagehands sat on the rear edge of the drum riser. They were partially hidden from view behind a stack of amplifiers. As the lights swept over them they changed appearance. It was momentary, but when the lights hit them, their dirty black garb changed. The clothing melted away and turned technicolour. Anaïs moved upstage in the wings to get a better look. The security guard followed her like a dutiful dog.

The lights hit them again. This time the beams stopped and held their position. Now

Anaïs had a much clearer view. Not only did their clothing change under the lights but also their physical features. One of them had long, blonde hair, the other a jet-black, rag-doll coiffeur. A manic grin split the face of the dark-haired one. He shook his head wildly and waved his arms around in an odd fashion. Was he conducting an orchestra or mimicking beating a set of drums? The blonde's gestures were easier to discern. He was playing air guitar.

The lighting changed, dousing the stage in a bright red glow. The pair was transformed. They reverted to being two grizzled roadies. Clothed again in black and looking exhausted from lack of sleep, they were clearly bored. One of them yawned.

Anaïs was confused. What was going on? Shades could only be seen in reflections. Finding two of them together was also unusual. She moved to get a closer look. A hand clasped her shoulder and stopped her in her tracks. Irritated, she flicked her shoulder to shrug it off. It grabbed her once more. Had the potion worn off on the security guard?

She turned to check and was met with the scowling face of a woman. A very familiar face. It was the caretaker. It was Nan. The jig was up. Anaïs studied the dark look on Nan's face and calculated how long she would be grounded. What a disappointing turn of events. It was all going so well.

'What is that?' said Nan angrily.

Nodding at the sky, she pointed over Anaïs's shoulder, indicating the skyscraper. It loomed over the stage, the sleek form of its silver spike shooting towards the heavens.

'Ahem,' said Anaïs innocently. 'I believe it's the Empire State Building.'

Nan swore under her breath. Anaïs sighed. There would be hell to pay.

London

an and Anaïs loved London. It was such a vibrant city.

If there was one place in the world where you could let your hair down, it was the British capital. There was so much to do. In the few short months they had been there, they had painted the city purple more times than they could remember. However, this time Anaïs knew she had overstepped the mark. The look on her caretaker's face told her she had gone too far.

Nan sighed. 'Anaïs, why have you turned that cat purple?'

'I just wanted to see if I could do it,' said Anaïs innocently.

The caretaker inhaled deeply through her nostrils. 'Anaïs, you may be in the body of a five-year-old, but you don't have to act like one. Animals should never be toyed with. It's cruel.'

'But—' stammered the little witch.

'No buts. The fun's over,' said Nan sternly. 'Change it back now!'

'I can't.' Anaïs shoved her hands in her pockets.

The caretaker folded her arms. 'Why not?'

Anaïs shuffled her feet nervously and avoided looking up at her caretaker. 'It will have to wear off.'

'How long will that take?'

'I don't know,' said Anaïs sheepishly, staring at the ground and dropping her shoulders. 'I didn't ask him.'

'Him! The Apothecary!' exclaimed the caretaker. 'I told you not to see him again without me.'

'I didn't see him,' said Anaïs defensively. 'He sent it by courier.'

'That's it! No more computer privileges for you!' The caretaker knotted her brow. 'Or did you use your promptuary?'

Anaïs continued to eye the ground.

'Great!' said Nan. 'Next time I have contact with the Organisation, I'll ask them if there's any way to block some of its functions.'

Sulking, Anaïs glanced up at her caretaker. 'Fine,' she mumbled. 'I won't contact him without asking you.'

'That's better,' said Nan. 'Now, what are we going to do about the cat?'

The animal looked forlornly at its fur. It could not see purple, but was definitely aware its coat had acquired a different shade. It licked the knuckle of its paw and examined it for any change. Disappointed at the outcome, it pulled a pitiful face at the two women.

'Sorry,' said Anaïs to the cat. She bent to pick it up. The animal sprang out of her reach and shot around the corner.

'Fantastic!' cried the caretaker. 'Now you've scared it away!'

'I told you, it will wear off, Nan,' said Anaïs.

'I hope you're right. What if its owner decides to take it to a vet or something?'

Anaïs shrugged.

'How did you do it anyway?'

Anaïs pulled a small atomiser out of her pocket. 'With this. It's a spray.' She waved it in front of the caretaker's face.

Nan threw up her hands in defence. 'Don't

point it at me!'

'Jeez, Nan! It's not a weapon!' Anaïs retorted.

'I wouldn't be so sure of that.' Nan flicked her fingers at the little witch. 'Give it here!'

Reluctantly, Anaïs conceded and handed the little bottle to the caretaker.

'Thank you.' Nan dropped the atomiser into her coat pocket. Dusting her hands, she checked to see if they had changed colour. She narrowed her eyes at the little witch. 'Don't do it again, okay?'

Anaïs shook her head. 'I won't.'

Nan regarded the witch dubiously, not entirely convinced. 'Good,' she said slowly. 'At least I think so. I suppose I'll just have to give you the benefit of the doubt.'

Anaïs nodded. 'Thanks.' She sighed. 'I'm bored. What are we going to do?'

Nan took a deep breath. She exhaled loudly. 'Anaïs, I can't entertain you all the time.' The caretaker studied the witch's face for a moment. 'However, I can see that if I don't keep an eye on you, you'll get into even more trouble.'

Anaïs's shoulders slumped in submission.

'I did have a surprise for you,' said Nan. She gnawed on her bottom lip. 'But now I'm not so sure we should do it.'

The witch's interest was sparked. Her eyes lit

up. 'C'mon, Nan, please tell me. I'll be good.'

'I have tickets to a concert.'

'Really? Who?'

'I got them the legitimate way. They cost a fortune. Otherwise, I probably would decide we shouldn't go.' She narrowed her eyes. 'I'm still not sure I can trust you. Or that you deserve it for that matter.'

Anaïs implored her. 'Nan, please tell me.'

The caretaker brought a finger to her lips. 'Shh ... give me a moment, please. I still have to decide whether it's worth the risk.'

Anaïs knotted her brow. 'What risk?'

'The risk of you screwing things up.'

Anaïs pursed her lips. The caretaker eyeballed her and waited, letting her simmer in silence.

Deciding the witch had waited long enough Nan pulled two bookmark-sized sheets of thin white cardboard out of her coat pocket. She showed them to Anaïs. 'I have tickets to the Rolling Stones.'

Anaïs looked at the tickets, slightly disappointed. 'The Rolling Stones?'

The caretaker looked hurt. 'I thought you'd be pleased. You told me you liked some of the songs I played for you?'

'I do, but aren't they a bit old?'

'Who, the Stones? Old? Sure, they're not as

young as they used to be, but I'm certain they can still put on a great show.'

'If you say so,' said Anaïs. She took a ticket from the caretaker.

'I thought you'd be more excited,' said Nan.

'It's okay, I suppose.' Anaïs screwed up her face.

'Good, then we'll go.' She wagged a finger at the little witch. 'But you must promise to be on your best behaviour. I'd like to enjoy the concert without having to worry about you.'

'Worry about me? You don't have to worry about me.' Anaïs winked and smiled at the caretaker. 'I'll be an angel.'

Nan rolled her eyes. 'Yeah, right!' She looked down the street. 'First things first. We need to sort out your current magical mishap. Come on, angel, let's see if we can find that cat.'

Zebra Crossing

As they walked down the street Anaïs turned the concert ticket over in her hand. 'It says here the concert is in Hyde Park. Is that big?'

'Hyde Park, big? Yes, it certainly is. It's huge. I always meant to take you there. It's beautiful. I expect there will be about fifty thousand people at the concert, maybe more.'

Anaïs's eyes widened. 'Fifty thousand? Wow!' She scrutinised the ticket again and muttered to herself. 'That's a lot of naturals all in one place.'

'What did you say?'

'Oh, nothing,' said Anaïs. 'Just thinking out loud.'

Nan grinned at her. 'Don't do that too often. People will think you're strange.'

'I am strange,' said Anaïs flatly. 'I'm a witch.'

'Unfortunately there's nothing we can do about that. But you could at least try to act normal.'

Anaïs snorted. 'Normal! What's that?'

Nan ignored her reaction. She stopped and looked around in frustration. 'Where is that cat?'

'Forget the cat, Nan. It's gone. Believe me, it will be all right. The potion will wear off. He guaranteed it.'

The caretaker screwed up her mouth. 'His guarantees are about as good as yours.'

Anaïs pulled a face at her. They rounded a corner and stopped. Further down the street was a zebra crossing. A lone man was pacing backwards and forwards across it. He began at the gutter on one side of the street. He carefully measured his stride across the crossing, taking pains to avoid touching the white lines. Once he reached the opposite gutter he did an about-turn and repeated the exercise.

Anaïs frowned. 'What's he doing? Trying to stop traffic?'

'I don't know, but he doesn't look right in the head,' said Nan. 'Maybe we'd better get him off the road?'

The man stopped and looked up. He turned to face them. His spectacles glinted in the sun.

'No!' Anaïs grabbed Nan and ushered her quickly around the corner.

'What are you doing?' the caretaker protested. 'And what do you mean "no"? We should help him. He looks lost.'

Anaïs hushed her. 'He is lost. It's a shade, Nan.'

'A shade? How do you know?'

'No shadow,' said Anaïs. 'Let's go.'

'Wait a minute. Then that's even more reason to help him. You know what you're supposed to do.'

'Not now, Nan, I'm not in the mood. And he looks creepy.'

The caretaker rolled her eyes. 'He's dead. Of course he looks creepy.'

'I ... just ... I have a bad feeling about him.' Anaïs flattened herself against the hedged fence to stay out of sight. A twig poked her behind the ear and she jumped away in surprise. She vigorously rubbed her skull where it had been scratched.

'Are you okay?' Nan went to inspect her head.

Anaïs jerked her head out of reach and nodded. 'I'm fine.'

The caretaker stepped back and looked Anaïs directly in the eye. 'Why the bad feeling? You only saw him for a split second.'

'It was enough. Look, I don't feel up to it. I know I should be practising this stuff, but not right now. Okay?'

Nan considered her for a moment. 'I think you're just making excuses again so you can get out of doing it.' She fixed the witch with a stern stare.

Anaïs averted her eyes. 'He's probably gone now, anyway.'

'Perhaps,' said Nan. She moved along the thick hedge, leaned forward and peered around the corner. The shade had resumed pacing across the zebra crossing.

A car swept past the women. It barely slowed as it rounded the corner, before barrelling down the street towards the pedestrian crossing. The driver saw the shade at the last minute and braked.

Upon hearing the squealing tyres, the shade looked up. Moments before car and shade connected, he coiled his body and leapt into the air. He sprang incredibly high, more than his own height, but not high enough to completely avoid the vehicle. His ankles clipped the leading edge of the car's roof. The force flipped his legs up into the air. His torso slammed into the centre of the roof. He bounced off the thin metal as if it were a trampoline. His legs did a full rotation around his body and he landed feet first where he had originally been standing. The car careened over the crossing before screeching to a standstill.

The shade appeared unharmed. Dumbfounded, he stared at the vehicle. The driver cranked open his door. The shade snapped out of his trance. He did a half-turn and sprinted across the road. He mounted the footpath, leapt a low fence and disappeared from view.

The driver got out of his vehicle and looked around, disconcerted. He walked back to the crossing. Finding nothing, he scratched his head and returned to his car. He inspected the roof of his vehicle. There was a small dent in the centre. He ran a hand over the indentation and rubbed the stubble on his chin. He glanced around the street, shrugged and got back in the vehicle. He drove off slowly.

'Weird,' said Nan. 'Did you see that?'

Anaïs stood between the caretaker and the hedge, her head nestled in Nan's armpit. 'Yes, I saw all of it.'

'Shouldn't we go check on the shade?'

Anaïs shook her head. 'No, I'm sure he's gone. The last thing I want to do is go chasing shades. Hopefully it will teach him to stop prancing around on zebra crossings.'

'You have no heart.'

'What do you think I'm supposed to do, Nan? I can't spend all day trying to sort them out.'

'You could at least put in an effort to help one of them. You have to start doing this sometime. You know it's what you're here for.'

'I know, but, like I said, I didn't feel right about that one.'

Nan pursed her lips. 'I don't get it.'

'You wouldn't.' She grinned at the caretaker. 'But then you're not a witch. Anyway, I'll choose to help when I feel like it.'

'I don't think that's the right attitude,' said Nan, disapprovingly.

Anaïs grunted. 'You say that about a lot of things I do.'

'No, I don't,' Nan countered. 'But I do think you should be doing more than just playing around with magic. You should do something useful with it.'

Anaïs sighed. 'You know I'm still learning, Nan. Give me a break. When I'm ready I'll help one of them. Just not now.'

The caretaker raised an eyebrow. 'Well, I think you're ready. You need to stop mucking around. It disappoints me that you're not doing the basic thing I taught you. You should help people.'

Anaïs waved her aside. 'I'll get there. Just give me some time.'

'Fine,' sighed Nan. 'But we haven't got forever.'

'I have,' said Anaïs. 'Sort of.'

'You'd better hope so. Although, I doubt you have an eternity. Forever is a very long time.'

They were interrupted by the howl of a dog in the distance. The two women looked at each other.

Nan furrowed her brow. 'You think that's the shade causing more trouble?'

Anaïs shrugged. 'Who knows? Like I said, not my problem. Let's just go.'

Going It Alone

Nan and Anaïs began the long walk back to their apartment. They had only reached the next corner when Anaïs stopped the caretaker.

'Nan?'

The caretaker looked down at the little witch. 'Yes, Anaïs, what is it?'

'Um ... I know it's asking a lot.' She hesitated and then measured her words carefully. 'Do you think I could have some time to myself? You know, do a bit of exploring? We have a couple of hours before the concert, don't we?'

She pulled the ticket out of her pocket and

checked the details.

'I don't know,' Nan replied. 'The park is pretty far away and it will take us some time to get there. Anyway, first I need to get something from home.'

Anaïs looked up at the caretaker with doe eyes. 'I could get to the park by myself.'

Nan tilted her head to one side, knitting her brows. 'By yourself?'

Anaïs nodded enthusiastically. 'Yes! C'mon, Nan! I've been out on my own before. I'm not a child.'

The caretaker regarded her with scepticism. 'To most people you look like one.'

Anaïs dropped her eyes and stared at her feet. She wore tiny rubber rain boots. They had brightly coloured stars stamped on them. *Curse the baby clothes!*

'I know what I look like to most people,' she muttered. She lifted her chin and drew in a deep breath. 'But I can take care of myself.'

The caretaker sighed. 'I know that. That's not what bothers me.' She flicked her thumb over her shoulder. 'I just caught you painting a cat purple. What's going to stop you doing other stuff like that?'

The little witch hunched her shoulders. 'I suppose you'll just have to trust me?'

'I'm a nanny,' said the caretaker drily. 'I trust nobody.'

Anaïs laughed. She waved her hands behind her head and rolled her eyes. 'Ooh, I'm shaking in my shoes.'

Nan folded her arms and frowned.

Anaïs stopped mocking the caretaker and attempted to pull a serious face. 'Fine, I'll be on my best behaviour.' She grinned as sweetly as she could, giving her best impression of an innocent child. It came out all wrong, as if she were baring her teeth like a dog.

Nan knitted her brow. 'Stop doing that. It doesn't work. You know I see through it.'

Anaïs stopped smiling and covered her teeth, bringing her bottom lip up over her top one. The dog impression remained. Anaïs stared at the ground and mumbled, 'It works sometimes.'

Nan twisted her own lip. 'Hmm ...' She ran her eyes slowly over the witch. 'I guess I could use a bit of time to myself as well.'

Anaïs shoved her hands in her coat pockets and waited for the nanny to continue. She drew a line on the footpath with the toe of her boot.

'If I let you go, where will we meet?' enquired the caretaker cautiously.

'At the concert,' said Anaïs, keeping her eyes to the ground.

'There will be heaps of people.'

'Trust me, Nan. I'll be safe on my own. I'll be careful.' She looked up and met the caretaker's gaze. 'How else am I supposed to learn anything if you don't let me try to do stuff alone?'

Nan considered her for a moment.

'You do have a point. Still, I'm not completely comfortable with it. You haven't been that far away from me before.'

'Think of it as a little test. It's only for a couple of hours.'

'How will I find you?'

'I'll find you.' Anaïs pulled out her promptuary and held it up in front of the caretaker's face. 'My handbook will find you.'

'I know it will, but I'd prefer to know where you are.'

'Look, if it makes you feel any better, I'm still wearing this.'

Anaïs slipped the promptuary into her pocket and extracted a silver necklace from her blouse. Dangling from it was a little talisman. She held it in her open palm and showed it to the caretaker. The jewel encrusted in its centre flashed. The miniature pinpoint of light it emitted blinked on and off at regular intervals.

Nan studied the light flashing on the talisman. 'Okay, fine, you're right. If I need to, I can find you.' She crouched, took the little witch by the shoulders and gave her a stern look. 'This is a big thing, Anaïs. Off you go, but be careful. And most of all, be good.'

Anaïs grinned broadly. 'You know I will!'

'I certainly hope so. Prove me right, Anaïs.'

A Journey Begins

Anaïs consulted her promptuary.

'Map,' she said.

The book obliged. The open pages transformed, depicting a plan of her immediate surroundings. A purple blip moved away from her. It was the caretaker heading back to their apartment.

She commanded the book, 'Show me how to get to the concert.'

The pages zoomed out and a new blip flashed in a far corner of the map. The park was, as Nan had said, quite some distance away. The promptuary shifted the focus of the map to the flashing point of light. It narrowed in on it. As the map magnified, Anaïs made out a bright green rectangle devoid of streets. The image enlarged further and she saw an area ringed by trees, with vehicles and a large square structure at one end. There was a hive of activity. A mass of people moved around the square structure like ants scattered around an anthill. The promptuary showed her great detail. She could even see the treetops swaying in the wind.

'Guide me there,' she instructed the book.

The map zoomed out to show a larger snapshot of the city. A purple line appeared. It zigzagged its way across the city of London, connecting her current position with that of the park. Anaïs frowned. It would take forever to get there with her little legs.

She murmured to herself, 'I think I'd better take a bus.'

She felt something rubbing on her lower leg and looked down. It was the purple cat. The animal raised its nose at her and twitched its whiskers. It meowed loudly.

'Sorry,' said Anaïs. She felt around in her pocket and wrapped her hand around a small cylindrical object. She pulled out the atomiser and opened her palm. She smiled. She had slipped the flask out of the caretaker's pocket when Nan had been distracted by the shade.

'Nan is going to kill me for this,' she said to the cat. The animal licked a paw and cleaned its whiskers. It eyed its paw and turned its head to the little witch. It meowed again.

'Sorry, I really can't help you,' said Anaïs, looking sorrowfully at the cat. 'Don't worry. It will wear off. I promise.'

The cat scowled at her, scratched the ground and raised its hind quarters. It turned and directed them towards her leg.

'Hey!' Anaïs jumped away from the animal. 'Give me a break! I told you it would wear off!'

The cat eyed her, sat down and proceeded to clean its crotch. Anaïs screwed up her nose and shook her head. Cats! She dropped the atomiser in her pocket. She consulted the map and looked around the street to get her bearings. At the far end was a bus stop. She headed off towards it. She threw a glance over her shoulder at the cat as she walked away. It was still engrossed in preening itself. *Good, just keep doing that.*

At the bus stop she stood in line behind an old woman and a punk. His lips, nose, eyebrows and ears were studded with piercings. He sported a purple mohawk. Anaïs grinned at him. He turned his back on her. *Sorry, I was just admir-*

ing your hair. One day I'm definitely gonna get myself one of those!

'Are you all right, child?' The old woman leaned on her wheeled shopping bag and looked at the little witch with concern. 'Where's your mother?'

If only I knew, thought Anaïs. She straightened, adopting a self-assured stance. 'She's waiting for me at the other end.' She smiled sweetly.

The woman eyed her with suspicion. 'You're very young to be travelling alone.'

'Oh, I do it all the time,' said Anaïs nonchalantly. *Please mind your own business, lady.*

The woman waved a finger at her. 'You know, it's very dangerous in this city, especially for small children. Every day I read about one of them going missing.' She trained her eyes nervously over the punk. 'Are you sure your mother knows you're here?'

'Yes, she does.' Exasperated, Anaïs sighed. 'Lady, would you mind giving it a rest? I'd just like to catch the bus.'

The old woman sniffed and drew in her breath sharply. 'Well, I never!'

The punk looked at Anaïs out of the corner of his eye and smirked. She raised her eyebrows at him. He lifted his chin and drew in a deep breath. Staring across the street he fought to keep a straight face until the bus arrived.

London Bus

Anaïs followed the punk and old woman onto the bus. They swiped their travel passes across the scanner next to the door. The driver watched her get on. He opened his mouth to speak. *Please don't ask why I'm travelling alone.* Quickly, she cocked her head at the old woman and grabbed her by the sleeve.

'Here, grandma, let me help you with that,' said Anaïs, reaching for the shopping cart.

'You'll do no such thing,' spat the old woman. She swatted the little witch's hand away.

Anaïs shrugged her shoulders at the driver.

He looked at her lethargically, closed the door and grunted. The bus pulled out from the kerb and trundled down the street. Anaïs squeezed past the woman and made her way to the rear of the vehicle. She mounted the stairs at the back. Upon reaching the upper floor she noted a decided chill in the air. Shades—lots of them.

She scrutinised the passengers. It was difficult to spot the dead, especially in the late afternoon on a bus. For the living, the summer warmth on the top floor was exceptionally good at provoking listlessness. They blended in seamlessly with the dead. All the passengers bore the same lifeless demeanour.

She searched for an empty seat. The upper floor was very full. The only spare seat was at the front next to a Japanese tourist. She walked down the aisle and climbed onto the seat beside her. The tourist looked up from her guide book and squinted out the window. She barely acknowledged that someone had sat down beside her.

Anaïs watched in silence as the streets glided by, gradually getting busier as they headed towards the centre of the city. Then the silence was broken. A male voice hissed in her head. *Are you a witch?*

Anaïs kept her eyes forward, focusing on the

road ahead. Maybe if she ignored it the shade would leave her alone.

Can you hear me?

Anaïs breathed out slowly. She glanced up at the face of the tourist beside her. The woman's eyes were glued to her guide book. She silently mouthed the words she was reading. She was alive. Shades are not that animated. In general they are static, at least facially. And she had never seen one of the dead reading. But there was a first time for everything.

She raised her eyes to the large mirror positioned above the front window. In it she could see the faces of most of the passengers. *Which one is it?* The mirror revealed all and levelled the playing field. In a crowd, spotting shades was often easier with their disguises intact. Usually, they carried themselves in a comatose fashion. The mirror cancelled this. Without their camouflages, shades were more active. They moved the same as the living. Some were easy to identify. Their dress sense gave them away. This was especially the case with one seated in the middle of the bus. He had clearly come from another century. The powdered peruke balanced on the shade's head was a dead giveaway.

I know you can hear me.

Anaïs bit her lip. She had not seen anyone speak. That is, if she discounted the girl in the far corner silently shouting the words to the song playing on her headphones. *Don't move,* she told herself. *It will leave you alone if you don't respond.*

The back of her head plummeted in temperature as if an icepack had been slapped across it. *Damn!* The shade was right behind her. Unfortunately, it was out of her mirrored sight lines. She could just detect the movement of a head in the lower corner of the reflection. It was crowned with wispy black hair which was teased, standing up on end. The breeze from the ineffective air-conditioning nozzle above her played over the bird's nest. Below the hair a scarf encircled its forehead. It was brightly coloured. Gaudy. She closed her eyes and held her breath. *Please go away.*

Don't be like that, it said. I need your help.

Anaïs tried to clear her head. Had he heard her? If she could hear the shade then there was every possibility he could do the same. She had no idea of their full capabilities. Did they only hear her if she directly spoke to them in her head, or could stray thoughts also be read? She didn't know. She opened her eyes and stared out the window before her. She focussed on her surroundings. Tall buildings, another bus, cars, bicycles, lots of traffic, nice sunny day, Tube station. *That's it!*

She had to get off. She might have considered helping the shade, but if she started with one, it would not end there. She would give herself away. They would all want attention. She would become a shade magnet.

Right now she had better things to do. She had to get to the concert on time. Otherwise, Nan would have her hide. If she showed up late the caretaker would never let her out alone ever again. Even this little bit of freedom was a stretch. Nan rarely let her do anything alone.

Anaïs slid off the seat. She kept her eyes focussed on the floor and moved towards the stairs. Something cold brushed her shoulder. *Is he trying to stop me? No chance of that, buddy!* She scooted down the stairs and waited at the bottom by the rear doors. From the corner of her eye she saw the old woman get up and move towards her. *Great! The living dead as well!* The bus slowed to a stop. She tapped the exit button furiously. *Hurry up! Open!*

The doors folded open and Anaïs jumped out. She looked towards the entrance to the station back down the street. A sudden cold spike froze her shoulder. He was trying to stop her. She flicked her shoulder, twisted her body and dived into the steady flow of people moving along the crowded footpath.

Tube Station

It was still there—the cold. Her entire spine was frozen. She had to shake him, but how? He was certainly persistent. She had to give him that.

She weaved through the throng, between the forest of legs on the footpath. She fixed her attention on her goal: the Tube station. He would not be able to follow her if the crowd thickened. The fact that he was still so close mystified her. *How was he so flexible? How did he fit?* She was small—very small. A five-year-old could fit into tight spaces. The shade may have been dead but he was still a full-grown adult. *How was he fitting through the little gaps between the living?*

Shades could touch the living. That had been one of the first lessons she had learnt about them. Naturals would feel what she felt, the frosty connection, the shiver running down their spines. Full body-to-body contact, however, could only occur if it was unintentional. As far she was aware, unless the contact was accidental, a shade would just bounce off. To her knowledge, they could not force their way through. Their camouflages, the sheens coating them, were real in the eyes of the living. There were limitations to the disguises. They were there for a reason. Brushing up against people was one thing, but passing completely through them was against the laws of the universe.

Right now, this was not her concern. She just had to get away. She didn't like this kind of attention. Being stalked by a shade was downright unpleasant.

She was fast. She could go faster. She dodged from side to side. She pushed herself. The crowd thinned. She broke into a sprint. *So you want to play a game?* People closed in around her again. She hunched over and made herself even smaller, although this hampered her running. *Go!* She dived headfirst between a particularly overweight woman and another loaded down with a mountain of shopping bags.

The chill across her shoulder blades dissipated. She heard a scuffle and a commotion behind her. The sound of a woman's shrill cry. Then a crash followed by glass shattering. She flicked her eyes over her shoulder. Bodies and groceries had hit the ground. *Yes! He collided with them. That should slow him down!*

She turned her attention to the station entrance ahead and did not dare look back again. Just keep going. *You've lost him.*

Anaïs rounded the last human obstacle, a street busker performing in front of the station. Leaping over his open guitar case filled with a collection of coins, she landed heavily. It broke her stride. She picked herself up and rushed across the station's foyer. She dropped to her knees, slid under the ticket turnstiles and clambered to her feet. Dusting herself off she glanced around to see if anyone had spotted her. The station attendant at the far end was too busy dealing with a woman, three children and a pram. Because of her perceived age she could travel for free, but she wanted to avoid questions. Even in a city as full as London a stray five-year-old would not go unnoticed.

She continued toward the escalators. As she descended, she turned and ran her eyes over the turnstiles. The apathetic commuter crowd filed through like cattle. They may have lacked vitality, but they were not dead. She could see no shades. More importantly, no one had a determined look in their eyes. No one was scanning the crowd for her.

She breathed a sigh of relief and sat down on the step. It was one of those incredibly long escalators which seemed to lead into the bowels of the earth. She could only just see the bottom. She pulled out her promptuary and opened it. She called for a map and the pages flickered and transformed.

'Show me my position,' she said.

A flashing spot appeared. Anaïs surveyed the map and tried to get her bearings. She did not have far to go. *Three, maybe four stops, and I'm there. I told you, Nan. There's no need to worry. I can do this alone.* She squinted at the plan of the city. *Where was Nan anyway?*

Anaïs spoke softly to the book. 'Where is Nan?'

The map zoomed out and a purple blip appeared. The caretaker was leaving their apartment.

'So much for lots of time alone,' Anaïs muttered. She closed the handbook and put it away. She hugged her knees and watched the advertising billboards whiz by above her head. A wisp of warm air swept down the escalator. It suddenly cooled. She wheeled around. The only people in sight were a clump of commuters several storeys above her. Somewhere behind them the shade had mounted the escalator. *Was it really the shade? It could be nothing. Better not tempt fate. Just keep moving.*

She stood, scampered down the last few steps to the bottom and rushed down the corridor.

The Underground

The London Underground gave her the heebie-jeebies. Ever since she had seen a film with Nan, she could not shake the image of a lone man being chased through the snaking tunnels. The film was old, but the suspense still worked. *An American Werewolf in London* had left a lasting impression on her. She did not know why it bothered her. She knew more than most. She could spot what was supernatural and what was not. She had no reason to be afraid. Werewolves did not exist. As far as she was aware.

Perhaps it was not just the horror film. The

tiled corridors made her feel uneasy. It was like being in a morgue. And if there was one place you did not want to be as a witch, it was a storage facility for shades. There were enough dead walking the streets without going to a guaranteed source.

Get over it. There's nothing to fear here.

She moved quickly. The chill she experienced on the escalator had evanesced. As she rushed through the tight corridors, the stifling humidity and stale air began to suck the life out of her. Short of breath, she slowed. Whoever had been tailing her would have trouble finding her down in the labyrinth. Of course, shaking one of them was only the start. There would certainly be more. The dead were always hanging around in the underground. Supposedly because residing below the surface brought them some form of comfort. Almost like a grave you could walk around in.

Just make sure none of them spot you. Keep moving and act your age. And don't think. It will only bring trouble.

She pulled out her promptuary and consulted it. *Not far now.* She put the book away, rounded a corner and ducked into an archway. It connected the main corridor to the platform. She flattened herself against the wall. Now, this was fun. She flicked her head from side to side. *Secret agent Anaïs Blue on the job. Working undercover.* Sometimes, being a kid was fun, especially when you had this sort of environment as your playground.

She slid along the smooth tiled wall to the corner. She stuck her head around it. *Is the coast clear? Yes, it is.* She stepped around the corner and flattened herself against the wall. She looked down the platform, narrowing her eyes. She continued in secret-agent mode. The station was deserted except for a group of suits at the other end. A rush of air signalled an oncoming train. *Excellent timing!* She would not have to wait.

The train entered the station. Its carriages hurtled by, buffeting her with wind. She bent her knees slightly and coiled herself for action. The train hissed to a halt. Automatic doors swished open right in front of her. She scanned the platform once more for possible assailants. Using the wall as a launching pad, she pushed herself away. She zipped across the open ground of the platform, no man's land, and jumped inside the train.

The carriage was full. She collided with the hard edge of a briefcase. *Ouch!* Thankfully it had not hit her in the face, but it had been close. She sighed and rubbed her breastbone.

Back to reality. Game over.

The owner of the briefcase shuffled wordlessly to one side. She slipped her hand though the gap between the bodies and closed her palm around a pole. Looking over her shoulder, she watched the doors close. Before they sealed completely she heard a familiar sound. The loud howl of a dog. Her eyes widened. *Yes, that was definitely a howl.* Curiously, it was the same howl she had heard earlier, just after she and Nan had seen the shade at the zebra crossing. *Strange! There must be more than one dog in London. A disturbing thought struck her. Maybe there really are werewolves in London?*

Commuting

Great! Rush hour. Immaculate timing, Anaïs!

The bus had been heaven compared to this. At least she'd had somewhere to sit. In the carriage it was standing room only. Commuters were crammed in shoulder to shoulder, with barely any breathing space. The train stopped at the next station. The passengers jostled around. A singular mass of flesh and blood rotated to allow people on and off. Anaïs had managed to inch closer to the pole and secure herself. She hugged it. She grimaced as her neighbours knocked against her, squirming to make room for themselves.

The train left the station and roared into the tunnel. The noise was deafening. Due to the hot weather, every window was open. Hot air poured in, along with the cacophony of screeching metal.

Worst of all was the smell. Not just the dank odour of the tunnel being pumped in through the windows, but the stifling reek of human sweat. She was soaked in it herself. The moment she stepped into the carriage, it had coated her. She could cope with her own odour, but it was the other occupants which bothered her. Being vertically challenged, in a five-year-old body, she was tucked under people's armpits. Not a fortunate position to be in on such a hot day.

The train shunted violently to one side as it transferred to another set of rails. The passengers were thrown about and she almost lost her footing. Practically crushed, she became the meat in a businessman sandwich. She elbowed them and they grunted apologies. Then she spotted it through a gap in the crowded carriage as everyone shifted position. There he was, the shade with the blackbird's-nest hair.

Initially she caught his reflection in the window. Had she not glimpsed that she would have failed to recognise him. He blended in perfectly with his surroundings. His camouflage was very different to what lay beneath. He was in the guise of an ordinary businessman. Dressed in an expensive suit, his hair cropped short, the only sign of what lay underneath was the brightly coloured bow tie around his neck. It had the same pattern as the scarf which was wrapped around his true forehead.

How did he get here?

In the reflection she saw his eyes roam the carriage. She made herself even smaller behind the cover of the human wall surrounding her. She looked up at the signage above the door. *Where are we?* Lights embedded in the map of the subway system indicated they were close to her destination.

Good, two more stops. Not far now.

She still had to get off without his seeing her. *Did he follow me onto the train? No, impossible. He hadn't been on the platform.* She was certain of that. He must have got on after her. Maybe he was not even looking for her anymore. Maybe it was just coincidence. No matter, she had to keep an eye on him. If he spotted her he would certainly be on her trail once again. She had to stay hidden.

She looked at the reflections of the other passengers in the windows. She compared the mirrored images with the occupants themselves. There were other shades. She could make out at least half a dozen in the carriage. She saw several women of various ages. Under her disguise, one was decked out in a sixteenth-century ballgown. She wondered how the woman could possibly fit in the crowded carriage with her wide hooped skirt. Anaïs cocked her head around her neighbour's leg. *What was the image the rest of the world saw?* The camouflaged version of the woman had a particularly wide girth. *That would explain it.*

There were also several men and, to her surprise, a small boy. She felt sorry for him. He was a shade she would be prepared to help if it wasn't for all the others. That is, if she knew how to help. Her experience was extremely limited. She was still trying to get a handle on it all. She had not really had the opportunity to put her knowledge properly into practice. The Organisation had advised keeping a low profile until they deemed her training had been sufficient. She was sure she already had all the preparation she needed. They may be right, though. If she was not careful she would be inundated by shades requesting assistance. Maybe that was the point. She had to learn how to manage her clients. Still, it was frustrating. Having a talent and not making full use of it was a crime as far as she was concerned.

Thankfully, none of the shades were in her immediate vicinity. When the train arrived at her station she should be able to slip out unnoticed. She only had to watch out for him. She had to make sure she was not spotted. He knew what she was.

The train lurched around a tight corner, once again throwing all the passengers to one side. She steadied herself on the pole. *What's the big hurry! Do underground train drivers take a secret pleasure in making everyone's journey unpleasant?* The carriage entered a station. Her ears popped with the change of pressure. She waggled her finger in one of them. She flexed her jaw to get some balance back into her ear canals. She glanced up at the rail plan above her. It was her station. *Right! Let's get the hell out of here!*

The train stopped and the automatic doors slid open. Nobody moved. *Is it just me getting out?* She grunted and forced her way to the door, prodding the businessmen in sensitive places to get them to move. *Ha!* If only they knew she had the insights of someone much older than a five-year-old. She gave them a look of pure innocence as they looked down at her with irritation. *Idiots!* One of them stood in the doorway, blocking her way. He refused to budge. She jabbed him in the groin with the sharp point of her elbow. The man puffed loudly, groaned and doubled over. *Oops! Your own fault, buddy!* She smirked.

She slipped out of the carriage and looked down the platform to get her bearings. The doors closed. At the last minute, from the door at the other end of the carriage, a businessman stumbled out. A man dressed in an expensive suit with a brightly coloured bow tie.

Oh, come on! Give me a break!

Avoiding The Dead

The train sped out of the station, the whir of its wheels and whine of its engine increasing in pitch and volume as it accelerated. Then there was silence. Visions of *An American Werewolf in London* returned to haunt her. Except, he was no werewolf, and would not tear her limb from limb. At least, she hoped not.

What does he want? Why won't he leave me alone?

She stared down the platform at him. He stood stock still, glaring at her and contemplating his next move. She did the same. There were a lot of exits in the long, sweeping tiled wall. *Hmm, they probably only lead to platforms.* She could go through and jump on another train, but then she would have to time it perfectly. She trained her ears, but couldn't hear another one coming. Silence. She had to act first while she had the slight advantage. If she moved quickly she would have a head start. Behind her was a staircase. There was another at the other end. The signage indicated it was the exit she should take. But if she chose that route she would have to get past him first.

Could he actually stop me? Hmm, doubtful. Where's Nan when I need her? She would know what to do.

She decided to hope for the best. She had lost him in the crowd before. She could do it again. *You just need a crowd. Then find one!* She wheeled on one heel and sprinted for the stairs behind her. *Damn these little legs! Why don't they go faster?* She hit the stairs and climbed them. *If only these puny stumps were longer I could do two at a time.*

At the first landing she glanced over her shoulder. He had not reached the foot of the staircase. *Keep going!* She mounted the next set of stairs and trained her ears for footfalls. She heard nothing, but that could be immaterial.

Do shades even make a sound? Another landing. Still no shade below. *Good!* Another set of stairs. *Will they ever end?*

She kept her eyes forward and concentrated on the steps ahead. *Falling is not an option.* The next section of floor rose to meet her eyes. It was not another landing. A long stretch of corridor. *Aargh! Go away, American Werewolf!* Still no sound behind her. *Forget it! Just keep going!*

She reached the top and rushed down the corridor. It was curved and she could not see what lay around the corner. *Man! This corner goes on forever. Keep moving.* The corridor straightened out. At the end she spotted the foot of an escalator. *No! The steps aren't moving!* She looked for another way out. There was none. *No other option ... Do it!*

Anaïs reached the bottom of the escalator. The first few steps lay flat against one another before developing into proper stairs. It was a long way up. Her shoe hit the first metal plate and she heard a sound. The clanking of machinery winding up. The stairs slowly began to move. *Thank god for the modern magic of sensors and automation!*

She panted. Stopping for a moment, she breathed through her nostrils, trying to slow her thumping heart. *Get as far away as possible. Keep going!* She mounted the stairs but it was hard going, much worse than before. Each tread was higher than the normal stairs below. She had to stretch her small legs to mount each step. The conveyer belt running along the top edge of the escalator was just out of reach. Or was it? *You can do it.* She jumped and grabbed hold of it. She let it drag her up. But she couldn't hang on. She was spent. She let go. She slumped on the step and twisted around, staring at the foot of the escalator. Mercifully, it was already a long way down. If he was still behind her she had managed to put some distance between them.

A movement in the shadows at the bottom caught her eye. *Oh no!* She pumped air into her lungs. *Bah! Underground air.* She dragged herself wearily to her feet and turned to mount the stairs. The full force of the setting sun hit her in the face and momentarily blinded her. The gentle rush of a cool breeze played on her face. She was at the surface.

The Park

Outside, in front of the station, the road was wide and busy, clogged with traffic. Beyond it, on the other side, was the park. There was another place she could hide. In the park she would be safe. Very soon Nan would be there.

Curse the shade. She had wanted time alone to explore and have some fun. That idea had misfired and fallen flat. *Thank you, whoever you are, for giving me this gift. Not! Curse being a witch! Give a girl a break! I don't want to spend the rest of my life looking over my shoulder.* She wiped the sweat from her brow and examined the back of her hand. It was coated in black grime. *London, city of smog.*

She moved away from the entrance to the station. *This concert better be good.* There was a set of traffic lights and a crossing further down the footpath. She pulled out the promptuary and opened it.

'Red,' she said, and trudged despondently over to the pedestrian crossing.

The traffic lights flickered and changed colour. The traffic screeched to a halt. A large truck had problems slowing in time. Its air-brakes hissed in protest and it almost back-ended a small black car standing at the stoplights. Dragging her feet, she crossed the road in front of the little car. She glanced at it as she passed. She could have sworn the vehicle's headlights followed her like eyes.

Stop imagining things.

She hurried over to the opposite footpath. In front of her was the entrance to the park. She slipped between the wrought-iron gates. Inside was an ancient oak tree with a massive trunk. She scampered around it and peered back across the road at the station entrance. A businessman appeared. *Is it him?* She looked at the ground beneath his feet. *No shadow. Yep, it's him.*

He stood on the footpath, swaying on the spot, his arms hanging loosely by his sides. Even with the camouflage she sensed his dejection. *Good, now it's your turn to be frustrated. Stupid shade!* The lights changed and traffic flowed between them. A river of metal which would be impossible for him to cross. *That should keep you busy for a while.*

Moving further into the park, she kept the tree between her and the shade's line of sight. Then she heard the roar of a crowd. *Strange, I didn't hear it before. Must have been the traffic.* She smiled. *At least it should be easy to find the concert.*

Anaïs followed the sound. It grew louder as she got closer. From the noise it was clear there were thousands of people. She picked her way through the trees and came face to face with a security fence. She walked along it until she stumbled onto a wide pathway. It was filled with concertgoers. She was quite close to the entrance. A transit van zipped down the side of the path. She had to jump back into the bushes to avoid being hit by it. *Man, what's the hurry?*

She stepped back out onto the pathway and let the flow of the crowd carry her towards the entrance. Security barriers funnelled the concertgoers single-file into a series of corridors which snaked their way to the main gates. People shuffled along like sheep being fed into a barn. *The living can do a pretty good impression of the dead if they want to. This is going to take forever!*

She ducked down low and wound her way between the forest of legs. She squeezed through the gaps in the crowd barriers. It was a tight fit, but being in a five-year-old body made it relatively easy going. She headed in a direct line towards the entrance. Down on her knees she could just make it out. In no time she pressed her way through the last barrier and stepped out into a more open area.

Security personnel were dividing the crowd and directing groups into corridors running perpendicular to the entrance. She slipped in behind a family with young children and followed them to where bouncers were searching people's bags.

A particularly large security guard with a friendly face indicated she should stop. Then a thought dawned on her. *Do I even have a ticket?* She pulled out her promptuary and thumbed through the pages. *Yes, there it is.* Nan had given it to her. She held it up in the security guard's face.

He frowned, looking first at the ticket and

then at the girl before him. 'Where are your parents?'

'My parents?' She looked for the family she had been following. They had already passed security and proceeded into the concert area. *Damn!*

'Yes, your parents or a guardian. Are you lost?'

'Lost?' She shook her head vigorously. 'No, of course not.'

'You can't come in unattended.' The guard scratched his forehead. 'How old are you anyway?'

'Older than I look,' she said and screwed up her face. *Unattended! What am I—a dog?*

'That may be so, but you certainly don't look anywhere near eighteen to me. Unless, of course, you can prove it, which I find doubtful. We have rules. I'm sorry, but if you're under a certain age I can't let you in unaccompanied.'

'My caretaker will be here soon,' she said defiantly.

'Then you will have to wait for them.' He folded his arms and looked down his nose at her.

Wait? I don't want to wait. She looked around and weighed up her options. *Curse this body.* She could play it safe and wait, but she wanted to get in there. Now she had ditched the shade she could finally have some fun. *Time to turn on the waterworks.*

She bit her bottom lip as hard as she could without drawing blood. It hurt and she burst into tears. She blubbered, sobbing loudly. 'I'm sorry. You're right. I am lost.'

The severe look on the guard's face softened. 'It's okay. I'll get you some help.' He placed a hand on her shoulder. 'Why didn't you tell me straight away?'

She shrugged and wiped her face with her sleeve.

'Come on,' he said, winking at her. 'This way.' He guided her through the main gates. Just inside the entrance a small caravan nestled up against the security fence. In front of it was a large parasol above a table and a few chairs. He sat her down at the table and pulled a chair up beside her. 'It's hot. Would you like something to drink?' He opened a cooler and produced a bottle of water.

'No, I'm fine,' said Anaïs, shaking her head. 'But thank you for helping me.'

He smiled broadly at her. 'No problemo.'

'What's your name?'

'Carl,' he said.

'Mine's Anaïs.'

'Nice to meet you, Anaïs. Are you feeling better now?'

'Yes, a little,' she said timidly. 'Thank you.'

Carl cracked the cap on the bottle. 'You should drink something.' He slid the bottle onto the table and laid the cap beside it.

'Maybe in a minute,' she said. She felt around in her pocket and found what she was looking for. She pulled out a small vial. It contained purple power sprinkled with white specks. She unscrewed the cap.

'What's that?'

'Oh, it's just something my caretaker gave me. It's really good and very refreshing, especially on hot days.' She poured the contents into the water bottle. It dissolved instantly. 'Try it.'

Carl eyed her with suspicion.

She urged him. 'Go on, you'll like it.'

He hesitated and then decided she was on the level. He put the bottle to his lips, took a deep swig and set the bottle back on the table. His face brightened. 'You're right. It is good.'

'I told you it would be.' She watched his face closely. Almost immediately his eyes glazed over. His shoulders slumped and he slouched in his chair. His head lolled to one side and he stared blankly past her.

She waved her hand in front of his face. There was no response. He continued staring into space and did not blink.

'Can you hear me?'

'Yes,' he mumbled, his voice slurred.

'Good,' she said. 'We're going for a walk.'

Carl nodded slowly and stood. She slid off her chair, stood beside him and took his massive hand in her own. She looked up at his face and smiled. 'Now, Carl, let's have some fun!'

Mind Enhancement

She indicated the bottle on the table. 'Carl? Don't forget your bottle.'

He let go of her hand and picked up the bottle. He screwed on the cap and dropped it in one of the pockets sewn into his trouser leg.

She grabbed both his hands and pulled him down to her level. Bending forward he stared vacantly at her, his face centimetres from her own.

She looked deep into his eyes. 'Carl? You are going to get thirsty every half an hour. Just take a sip from your bottle and you'll be fine.' She intensified her gaze. 'Do you understand?'

Carl licked his lips and nodded.

'Every half an hour, Carl,' she said forcefully. 'Do not forget.'

He blinked and spoke in a monotone voice. 'I will not forget.'

She gave him a half-hearted smile. *I hope you are a good listener, Carl.*

'Where does the water come from, Carl?'

'Over there,' he said, pointing over her shoulder.

She turned around. They were very close to the main stage. She grinned. *Cool!* The stage had been designed to blend in with the thick line of trees running behind it. With a frame constructed of scaffolding, it bristled with lighting equipment and was decorated with fake foliage. The structure was flanked by two enormous speaker stacks.

High barriers with black netting separated the backstage area from the audience. Close to where they stood, a makeshift corridor had been created. It followed the line of the main security fence and connected them with the backstage area. A particularly large security guard filled the entrance to the corridor. *The man was almost as wide as he was high. I wonder if he will like Carl's water?*

'Anaïs!'

The sharp voice made her jump. She let go of Carl and spun around. 'Oh, hello Nan.'

'What's wrong with you?' The caretaker put her hands on her hips. 'I was calling out to you before. Why didn't you answer?'

'When?'

'Just before—outside. You ignored me and took off into the crowd.' She looked hurt.

'I'm sorry, Nan. I didn't hear you,' said Anaïs coyly. 'There are a lot people here.'

The caretaker scrutinised her, not entirely convinced by her excuse. She looked at the guard. 'Who is this?'

Anaïs grabbed him by the sleeve. 'This is Carl,' she proclaimed proudly.

'Carl?'

'Yes, he's helping me.' Anaïs held up his arm. 'Don't be rude, Carl, shake hands.'

Nan took his hand and shook it absentmindedly, keeping her eyes fixed on Anaïs. The guard held on for a little too long and Nan looked down at their hands.

'That's enough, Carl,' said Anaïs. He obliged, letting go of the caretaker's hand and dropping his arm.

Nan frowned. 'Surprisingly flaccid grip for a guard,' she muttered. She studied his face. He blinked and looked straight through her. 'What do you mean he's helping you?' she enquired, looking down at Anaïs.

'He's going to take me on a backstage tour.'

'Okay.' She eyed the guard. 'How do you know him?'

'We go way back.' She grinned mischievously and nudged him in the thigh with her elbow. Carl rocked on his heels and continued to stare into the distance.

'What are you talking about? You don't know anyone in London.' She studied his face again. 'What did you give him?'

'Oh, nothing,' said Anaïs innocently.

'Anaïs?'

The witch dropped her eyes and stared at her shoes. 'Just a little mind enhancer,' said Anaïs sheepishly.

'Mind enhancer! More like a mind bender.'

Anaïs breathed deeply through her nose. 'He'll be fine.' She gave the guard another nudge. 'Carl? Have a drink.' He pulled the water bottle from his trousers and took a swig.

'I certainly hope we're not going to have a purple-cat problem here,' said Nan gravely.

Anaïs shook her head. 'Of course not. That was experimental. This stuff is tried and true.'

'It better be,' said Nan.

'It is, and I have an antidote.' Anaïs fought to

maintain an air of innocence. *Not!*

'Good,' said Nan. 'Let's go then. It's getting late and I think the band will start soon.' She paused. 'And I really have to go.'

'Go?'

'Yeah, you know ... go.' Nan nodded at her pelvis. 'I was standing in line for ages.'

Anaïs smiled. 'Well, let's go then.'

Backstage

Getting past the wall of a man guarding the entrance to the backstage area had not gone as smoothly as she had hoped. After failing to get Carl to communicate properly, the guard had demanded to see security passes. In desperation she had grabbed Carl's bottle and thrown water into the other guard's face. It had worked, but Nan had not taken kindly to her actions, which had complicated things further.

Things had been much more manageable when she was alone. It was good that Nan was there, but not if she had to make excuses for everything she did.

'What are you doing now?' cried Nan.

'Shh! Just give me a moment.' Anaïs's eyes darted around to see if they were being watched. She frisked the pockets of the mammoth security guard. To her delight she found several backstage passes in the form of armbands.

'Here, take one,' she said, handing a pass to Nan.

The caretaker sniffed. 'Anaïs, I'm not at all comfortable with this.'

'C'mon, Nan!' she pleaded. 'It will be fine. Let's have a bit of fun.'

'I don't want to miss the concert. What if they kick us out?'

'They won't do that. Not now we have these.' She held up the backstage passes. 'And we have an extra insurance policy.'

'An extra insurance policy?'

'Yeah,' she said and flipped her thumb at the guard. 'We have Carl.'

An idiotic grin had spread across his face. Nan looked at him. She chewed her bottom lip. 'I'm not entirely certain he can provide much insurance.'

Anaïs sighed. 'Nan, please stop worrying.'

'I can't. It's my job.'

'Okay, fine, you do the worrying then. I'm

going to enjoy myself.' She took Carl by the hand. 'Come on, let's go. The longer we stand here the more chance that we draw attention to ourselves.'

She escorted Carl down the makeshift corridor and into the backstage area. Nan followed reluctantly, dragging her feet. Once they were into the area proper they were caught up in a hive of activity. Technicians and other personnel were running around making final preparations. Nobody batted an eyelid at them. *Good, it's working. Carl is good insurance.*

'Where are the toilets, Carl?'

He raised a limp-wristed arm and, without looking, indicated somewhere towards the rear of the stage.

'Off you go, Nan,' she said.

'Aren't you coming with me?'

'No, I'll wait here with Carl.'

'But—'

'You don't need us to take you to the toilet, do you?'

'I suppose not.'

'You have your pass,' Anaïs insisted. 'Look around. Nobody will bother you. They're all way too busy. We'll wait here.'

Nan surveyed the organised chaos. 'Okay, but don't go anywhere.'

'Of course not. I promise.' Anaïs crossed her heart.

'Where have I heard that before?' said the caretaker.

Anaïs rolled her eyes and puffed her cheeks in exasperation. 'Just go, Nan.'

The caretaker tramped her way along the side of the stage, occasionally having to dodge her way through the bustle. She disappeared into the crowd.

Anaïs's eyes roved around and then lit up. Lined up next to the stage were rows of trucks. Several of them had great cylindrical steel tanks mounted on them. Thick rubber hoses ran out of the bases of the tanks. She followed the line of the hoses. Some of them ran around to the front of the stage. Others circled around to the rear.

Anaïs pulled on Carl's sleeve and pointed at the trucks. 'Is that the drinking water?'

'No, it's a general water supply. We also use it to wet the crowd,' said Carl.

She raised an eyebrow. 'Wet the crowd?'

'It's hot. It keeps them cool.'

'I see.' She pondered the trucks for a moment. 'I have an experiment I want to try out.'

Carl nodded.

'Will you help me?'

Carl nodded again.

'Let's go then.' She took him by the hand and led him through the crowd and across to the trucks.

Spiking The Water

Anaïs climbed the tanker truck. She mounted a steel ladder which ran up the rear of the vehicle. Carl had set her on the bottom rung. Although she had no fear of heights, it was a precarious climb. At the top of the ladder she climbed onto the roof of the tank and sat down. It was better not to move too much. The shiny steel surface was very slippery.

From her perch she had a perfect view over the park. It took her breath away. There were so many people. Thousands of them were crammed into an area ringed by trees. On a normal day it would have been an empty field. Now it was fully packed. The sun was making its slow descent and she could see it hovering above the tree line. Twilight was approaching. *Perfect!*

She looked around the roof of the tanker. There was a large circular manhole with a small cap in its centre. She tried to screw it off. She grunted. It was a tight fit and she needed all her feeble five-year-old strength to pry it loose. With some effort she managed to unscrew it. Inside it was dark and she could not see the contents. She inhaled. The fresh waft of cool water drifted up her nostrils.

She felt around in her pocket and found the atomiser. She held it up in the sunlight. It looked so innocent. She had a moment of doubt. *Should I or shouldn't I?* She glanced around the backstage area. *If you're going to do it, then do it quick!* She opened the little bottle and poured the contents through the hole. She listened to the sound of the liquid hitting the water. The tank was very full.

Bah! She shook her head. *It probably won't work. It'll be too diluted.*

'Hey! What are you doing up there?'

The voice, coloured with a sharp American twang, came from below. She looked over the edge of the tank. A very small man, dressed entirely in black, stood at the foot of the ladder with his arms folded. He glared up at her. He was festooned with an innumerable number of backstage passes. They hung from lanyards around his neck. Tools, two walkie-talkies and other paraphernalia hung from his belt. He looked like a Christmas tree. She covered her mouth to stifle her laughter. *Hello, boss man!* She pursed her lips and mustered the most serious look she could.

'I'm with him,' she said, pointing down at Carl. The man looked up at the security guard beside him. Carl towered over him. He stared vacantly at his own reflection in the mirror-like surface of the steel tank.

Maybe I can get him to knock the guy out. No, Anaïs, don't be stupid.

The Christmas tree furrowed his brow. 'She's not allowed on there you know.'

Carl was blissfully unaware of everything, except his own reflection, and failed to react.

'Hey! I'm talking to you.'

Carl maintained his stoic gaze. The Christmas tree huffed in exasperation. He waved a finger at Anaïs.

'You're not allowed on there. Get down now!'

She flashed him her sweetest smile. 'Okay,

I'm coming.' She stuffed the little bottle into her pocket and climbed down the ladder. At the bottom rung she turned to face Carl. She jumped into his arms and slid down his body.

The Christmas tree had his hands on his hips and glowered at her. 'How old are you anyway?'

'Five.'

'Five!' He yelled at Carl. 'How can you let a five-year-old climb on the equipment?'

Carl blinked once, but other than that, did not respond.

She tugged on Carl's sleeve. He knelt beside her. She hissed in his ear. 'Carl, tell him I'm lost.'

Carl straightened. 'She's lost,' he said flatly.

The Christmas tree looked suspiciously at Carl and then at her. He bent forward, bringing his face uncomfortably close to her own. One of the walkie-talkies hanging from his belt squawked loudly. They both flinched at the sound.

'Dermot, ...ere are you?' The voice from the walkie-talkie was muffled by static and barely understandable. 'We're ...bout to start.'

Dermot straightened, cocked his head and spoke into the mouthpiece clipped on his collar. 'I'll be right there. Just sorting out a little problem.'

I may be little, but the problem won't be if you don't leave me alone.

Dermot snapped at Carl. 'Make sure you get her out of here!'

She nudged the security guard. Carl grunted. His head lolled forward.

Dermot pursed his lips and shook his head. 'Jeez, the people they hire here.'

The walkie-talkie squawked again. Dermot yelled with irritation into the mouthpiece. 'Okay, okay, I'm coming!'

He barked at Carl. 'Sort it out! I don't want to see her again!' He turned his back on them and stamped off towards the stage. She watched him leave.

Man! What an idiot!

She looked up at the security guard's face. 'Carl? Have a drink.'

The Building

Darkness had begun to descend. Nan was nowhere to be found. *Good!* thought Anaïs. *More time to myself.* She moved along the rear of the stage, picking her way over thick cables and other staging material. Guilt overcame her and she decided to check on her caretaker's whereabouts. She pulled out her promptuary. Before she could command it to find Nan a burly technician blocked her way.

'You're not allowed back here,' he said, eying her intensely.

'I'm lost,' she said. She tipped her head at Carl. 'He's helping me find my mother. Isn't that right, Carl?'

Carl looked down at her in silence. She whispered loudly out of the corner of her mouth. 'Nod your head, Carl.' The security guard obliged. The technician regarded him warily.

Her eye was caught by something shimmering over the technician's shoulder. 'Wow! What's that?'

Several metres away, in front of the tree line, stood one especially enormous tree. It was several storeys high.

'It's not real,' said the technician. 'It's a projection on a water curtain.'

'Impressive. It looks real. A water curtain?'

'Yes, instead of a normal screen, we make one out of water. We create a mist and then project images onto it, with this.' He indicated an enormous projector standing a few metres away. Her eyes wandered from the projector to the image. A breeze caught the water curtain and the giant tree wavered as if it was swaying in the wind.

'But it's huge!'

'Oh that's nothing,' said the technician with a smug look on his face. He glanced up at his handiwork. 'We once projected an image the size of the Empire State Building.'

Anaïs's eyes widened. 'The Empire State

Building!'

Bright light flashed from the open pages of the promptuary and almost blinded her. A pencil-thin blue beam shot from its spine. The ray of light hit the projection equipment. In an instant the image of the gigantic tree vanished. There was a cracking noise from the projector, almost like the snapping of a whip. The blue beam from the book disappeared. Intense light streamed from the lens of the projector. On the water curtain a glow formed. Light shimmered first at its base. It then shot up into the twilight sky. A full-size image of the Empire State Building materialised before her eyes. Anaïs's jaw dropped.

Fortunately, the technician was standing with his back to the equipment. He had turned his attention to Carl and had not seen the change in the projection. She quickly pulled her eyes from the apparition behind him.

'Is he okay?' enquired the technician, nodding at Carl.

Anaïs cleared her throat. 'Yes, he's fine.' She moved closer to Carl and grabbed his sleeve. 'I think we'll be going now.'

The technician looked down with curiosity at the promptuary. 'What was that flash of light? Did it come from your book?'

'Flash of light? Carl, did you see a flash of light?'

Carl stared into space.

'I saw no flash of light.' She cocked her head at the security guard. 'I don't think Carl did either.'

The technician was unconvinced. He narrowed his eyes and held out his hand. 'Can I have a look at it—the book?'

She stepped away from him, sheltering behind Carl's arm. 'No,' she said, shaking her head vigorously. 'I don't think so.' She shut the promptuary and put it away. 'I'm sorry. We should go.'

'Really? Are you sure?'

'I need to keep looking for my mother.'

'I understand,' he said, slightly disappointed. 'It's a pity, though. It's nice to have some company. It's as boring as hell here.'

She grinned at him. 'Well, I hope it livens up for you.'

He smiled. 'Fat chance of that!'

'Well, you never know.' Her eyes wandered to the huge image behind him. She quickly pulled them away and looked up at the security guard. 'Carl, let's go.'

'Anyway, nice to meet you,' said the technician.

'Nice to meet you too,' she replied.

She took Carl's hand and led him along the rear of the stage. The technician watched her leave. She turned and waved goodbye to him, once again avoiding looking at the enormous projection behind him. As they slipped around the corner, Anaïs breathed a deep sigh of relief.

BUSTED

The cacophony onstage was overwhelming. The caretaker had found the little witch and spotted her handiwork. Nan knelt beside Anaïs. She had to yell in her ear to make herself heard above the din of the band.

'How are you going to get rid of it?' she pressed the little witch, nodding at the skyscraper looming over the stage.

'I don't have to get rid of it. It's just an illusion, Nan,' said Anaïs. She crossed her fingers behind her back. *Please don't ask me to do something about it. I have no idea how to get rid of it.*

'Illusion or no illusion, it shouldn't be there, should it?' Nan frowned at her. 'What if the Organisation finds out about it? They will have my hide.'

'Pff! Organisation! Like I care,' said Anaïs.

'You may not care, Anaïs, but you know the rules,' Nan said seriously. 'We're supposed to keep a low profile. You know you're not allowed to do this sort of thing.'

The little witch protested. 'I was just having some fun.'

'You need to think about other people, Anaïs. Me, for one,' said Nan. 'If she finds out, my mother won't take too kindly to this.'

'I thought you didn't care what she thought?' said Anaïs, twisting her mouth.

'I don't, but I can't avoid her wrath. As head of the Organisation she won't let me off lightly. And you know as her daughter I come under more scrutiny than anyone else.'

Anaïs shrugged. 'Let her do her worst.'

A look of concern cast a shadow across the caretaker's face. 'I don't think you want to see that, Anaïs,' she said grimly.

Nan looked out into the audience. The first ten rows were curiously static. With rigid shoulders, they swayed on the spot, their mouths agape, staring at the stage. They were not looking at the projection above it.

She lifted her chin towards the crowd. 'What's up with the people down there?'

Anaïs's eyes wandered around the stage. 'They're … ahem … seeing something else,' she said with an air of innocence.

'Something else?'

'Purple.'

Nan folded her arms and frowned. 'Purple? What do you mean "purple"?'

Anaïs shuffled her feet. She avoided looking the caretaker in the eye, focussing instead on the scaffolding above them.

Nan growled at her. 'Anaïs?'

The little witch sighed. 'The water. I put something in the water. Sort of an experiment. To be honest, I didn't even think it would work.' Anaïs grinned. 'But it did. I think I actually pulled it off.'

'Great!' Nan groaned. 'That's it! I don't want you communicating with the Apothecary again. He's more trouble than he's worth.'

'Oh, c'mon,' Anaïs whined. 'He's great! He comes up with the coolest stuff.'

'Anaïs, this has to stop. Drugging people all the time is not being responsible.'

'It doesn't hurt them. It wears off.'

'That may be so, but it bothers me. What

happens when it wears off and these naturals find out what they've done under the influence of your concoctions?'

'I just made them see another colour.' She looked out over the crowd. 'What's the harm in that?'

'Enough of this, Anaïs! You know as well as I do we can't go playing with people's lives.' Nan began to turn red in the face. 'And you didn't just make them see another colour. You did that!' She threw her arm in the air, indicating the skyscraper.

'You're no fun.' Anaïs pouted.

The caretaker glared at her.

Anaïs relented. 'Fine! I get your point.'

'Good!' Nan breathed deeply. 'We can't play games all the time. Sometimes even I have to do stuff I don't like. Where's the potion?'

Anaïs looked at her sheepishly and reached into her pocket. She pulled out the little bottle.

The caretaker spluttered. She stared at the bottle in disbelief. 'That's the atomiser I took away from you earlier today!'

'I know,' said Anaïs. She dropped her eyes and stared at her feet.

'You took it out of my jacket!'

'Yes,' said Anaïs timidly.

Nan blew out a mouthful of air. 'Anaïs, how

am I supposed to trust you with anything? You stole from me.'

'I didn't steal from you. It was mine.'

'That's a matter of opinion,' said Nan, fuming. 'I confiscated it.' She held out her hand. 'Give it here!'

Reluctantly, Anaïs handed her the bottle. Nan held it up to the light. 'It's empty. What did you do?'

'I dumped all of it in the water supply.'

Nan shook her head. 'Anaïs, you can't do that. Anyone could drink it. You must never perform magic you can't control. Anyway, it was my understanding this was for spraying cats and not to be taken orally?'

'I thought I'd give it a shot. I didn't have any other magic and it seemed like a good opportunity.'

Nan puffed her cheeks and flared her nostrils. 'You could hurt somebody, Anaïs! You can't do stuff like this. It's dangerous.'

Anaïs nodded soberly. 'Sorry, Nan.'

'I don't think I'm the one you should be saying sorry to,' said Nan, studying the crowd.

A movement at the back of the stage caught the little witch's eye. Out of the shadows a figure appeared. A spotlight flicked over it as its beam panned across the curtains. Anaïs sucked in her breath. It was him—the shade in the businessman's suit.

Reunion

The businessman joined the two scruffy-looking road crew. As Anaïs watched, she saw the oddest thing. The stage lighting played gently over the three of them. Then a stroboscope ignited. With every punctuated flash of light they were stripped of their camouflage. The shades huddled together in a tight group. They slapped each other on the shoulders. They seemed overjoyed to see one another.

The businessman stepped away from the group and stared directly at her. She now saw his full attire exposed beneath his disguise. He wore high, black boots. They were partly covered by bell-bottom trousers which fanned out at his calves. A brightly coloured vest hung loosely over a white shirt with billowing sleeves. Wrapped around his head was the scarf she had seen before. It was a sort of bandana. He almost looked like a pirate.

The shade fixed her with a piercing stare. In the flickering lights his eyes had a look of desperation. Then the flashing stroboscope subsided. The lights panning over them stopped moving. They held their position, trapping him in their glow. She had been mistaken. His eyes were not harsh at all, they were soft—even kind.

He smiled at her and raised his arm. He made a fist. His thumb shot up like he was flicking a coin. He thrust his fist towards her. Then she realised what he was doing. He was giving her a thumbs-up.

She grinned and returned the gesture. He beamed back at her. In one deft movement, he slid his thumb down over his fingers and raised two of them, creating the shape of the letter V. She cocked her head. *What is that, a peace sign?*

The lights slowly dimmed. The shade's white teeth, made even brighter by his dark skin, shone in the shadows. He nodded a thank-you at her and turned to face the other shades. The three of them slung their arms around each other's shoulders. They pulled themselves into an embrace. The stage went completely black.

The roar of the crowd drew her attention. She looked out into the audience. They were screaming in unison with the lead singer. Mick Jagger stood on a stage monitor in a solitary beam of light, urging them on. For a moment she had forgotten where they were. The strange actions of the shades had completely held her focus. Her eyes wandered back upstage. *What were they doing now?*

The music built to a crescendo. Bright light suddenly illuminated everything, flooding the stage. She squinted and shielded her eyes with her forearm. The music died. There was a moment of silence. She peered out from under her arm. The upstage area was deserted. The shades were gone.

Nan whispered in her ear. 'Anaïs, I just saw the strangest thing.'

'So did I. What did you see?'

The caretaker scratched her head. 'I could have sworn I saw Jimi Hendrix, Brian Jones and Keith Moon having a group hug.'

'Who are they?'

'Oh, you wouldn't know them, but you should. They were very famous musicians. Unfortunately, they are long gone now.'

'I wouldn't be too sure of that,' murmured Anaïs.

'What? Did you say something?'

Anaïs shook her head. 'No.'

'So, what did you see?'

'Oh, nothing.' Anaïs shrugged. 'I think the light was playing tricks with my eyes.'

Nan nodded. 'Me too, I suppose.'

Did I just inadvertently help a shade?

On the opposite side of the stage she felt another set of eyes fall upon her. Shielding her eyes again with her forearm she peered across to the other side. *Oh no, trouble.*

She grabbed the caretaker by the elbow. 'Nan? I hope you've seen enough. It's time to go.'

'Why?'

'Just because ...' She watched the familiar sight of a man, decorated like a Christmas tree, moving around in the wings. Dermot began to make his way around the perimeter of the stage towards them.

Leaving

The caretaker consulted her mobile phone. Its screen lit up her face in the semidarkness.

'We have to go, Anaïs,' said Nan.

'I know.' She glanced at the ceiling. The floorboards rumbled with the muffled sound of the band performing above them.

'No, I mean really go—away.'

'Away?' Anaïs studied the caretaker's face. 'You mean from London?'

Nan nodded.

'Why?' moped Anaïs. She moaned, 'I like it here.'

The caretaker's eyes darted around the room. To avoid being confronted by Dermot, they had slipped under the stage. In the rush to get away from him they had lost Carl. Finding a deserted storage area, they had entered the room and Nan had secured the door. They had begun formulating a plan to get out of the concert area when the caretaker's phone had buzzed.

'Anaïs, we can't stay.' Nan scrutinised the message on her phone. 'The damage is done. We're too exposed here,' she said gravely.

'Exposed? What do you mean? I don't feel exposed.' She screwed up her face, rolled her eyes and flicked her head at the ceiling. 'Well, except for doofus up there.'

Nan held up her phone. 'The Organisation contacted me. They say you're not safe here.' She pursed her lips. 'It's not my choice. I like London too.'

'But I don't want to leave,' said Anaïs despondently. She dropped her eyes to the floor.

'We have no choice,' said Nan. 'Unfortunately, I fear you will have to do this more often.' She slipped her phone in her coat pocket and placed a hand gently on the witch's shoulder. 'Anaïs, a witch's lot is not an easy one. It's of great importance that you stay concealed from the outside world. I realise this will be difficult, especially as your job is to influence it, but you have to practise your magic without being noticed. Naturals can't know what we're up to.'

Anaïs tilted her head. She looked up at her caretaker inquisitively. 'Why?'

'Naturals will not accept you the way I do.' Nan crouched down, bringing her face level with the little witch's. 'Anything they find mysterious they will investigate and try to uncover. They're unable to leave things alone. Naturals are decidedly unnatural. They don't let nature run its course. What they don't understand—what they fear—they destroy.'

'That's terrible. Can't we stop them? Can't we let them know what they're doing is wrong?'

'Believe me, Anaïs, many have tried and failed. But we will not give up on them.' She gripped the witch by the shoulders and peered into her eyes. 'It's what we're here to do, Anaïs. It's what *you* are here to do.'

Anaïs frowned. 'Is there no way we can just move out to the suburbs? Then we can still visit the city sometimes. We won't bother anyone out there.'

Nan relaxed her grip on Anaïs. She shook her head. 'No. For a start there's no way I'm living in the suburbs. Anyway, I don't think you can influence the world from there. You need to stay hidden, but that doesn't mean you should run away and hide. I may be wrong, but I think you need to be in a central location to solve the heart of any problem.'

Anaïs shoved her hands in her pockets. She screwed up her face. 'But we are central here. Where is more central than London?'

A crashing sound came from outside. Then a loud thud, as if something heavy had been thrown against the door. Nan let go of Anaïs. She whipped around and stared at the door's solid metal surface. Even over the rumble of the band above she heard the huff of laboured breathing coming from the other side. Then there was an awful scratching. It sounded as though steel spikes were being dragged slowly down the full length of the door.

Anaïs grimaced at the piercing, high-pitched screech. She looked with alarm at the door and then up at her caretaker. 'What's that?'

Nan turned to Anaïs. Her eyes were clouded with fear. 'I don't think you want to know,' she said in a hushed whisper.

'What do you mean?' cried Anaïs.

The all-too-familiar howl of a dog sounded beyond the door.

Nan bent forward and grabbed the witch by the shoulders again. She fixed her with a stern look. She hissed at her. 'Enough talk, Anaïs. We have to go!'

'Where, Nan? Where are we going?'

The caretaker swept Anaïs up into her arms. She glanced furtively around the room. Spying another door at the far end, she sprinted towards it. Between gasps for breath she whispered loudly in the little witch's ear, 'To Amsterdam, Anaïs. The Organisation is sending us to Amsterdam.'

Get The Scoop

**Anaïs Blue's magical mishaps
did not go unnoticed.**
Reports are beginning to appear in the press.
Get exclusive access to the press
statements as they surface.

Go to
www.pjwhittlesea.com/anais-blue-press/
or scan the QR code to find out more.

Other books in the Anaïs Blue Series:

Thistle Witch: Anaïs Blue Book 1
Discovering Magic: Anaïs Blue Book 2
A New Source of Magic: Anaïs Blue Book 3
A Witch's Calling: Anaïs Blue Book 4
Magic Awakes: Anaïs Blue Book 5

Check tyetbooks.com or join the author's newsletter for updates on releases. Scan the code below to get access.

ALSO BY PJ WHITTLESEA
LORELESS

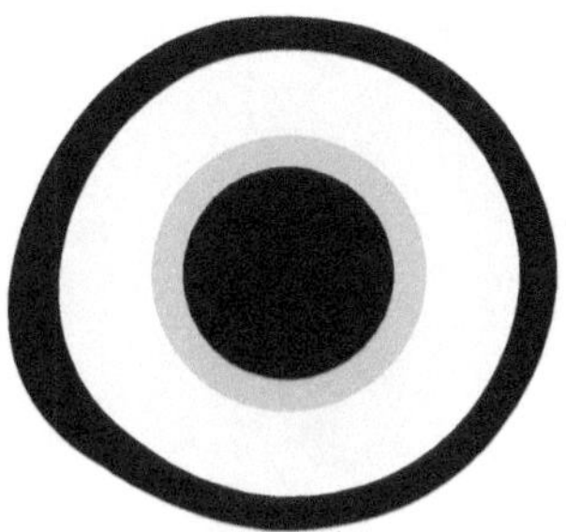

Have you ever wondered where you came from?

Take an inspiring journey into an Australia you never knew existed.

On the eve of his wedding, and through a bizarre set of circumstances, an Aboriginal urbanite finds himself stranded in the remote Australian outback.
In an effort to get home he embarks on a journey, not only into himself, but also into his heritage.

Part quest, part ghost story and part contemporary fable, Loreless combines magic, mysticism, wisdom and wonder into an inspiring tale of self-discovery.

Available in ebook, paperback and hardcover. Find out more at **www.tyetbooks.com**